W9-DCV-392

Disney
FROZEN

Let's Play
POP-OUT
Mask Book

Bath · New York · Cologne · Melbourne · Delhi
Hong Kong · Shenzhen · Singapore · Amsterdam

Anna

Princess Anna is smart, loving, and kind. She adores her big sister, Elsa, and wants to spend time with her. When Elsa gets into trouble, Anna leaps into action. She is very brave, and is always looking for a new adventure!

Ask an adult to help.

To remove your Anna mask,
tear the tabs along the perforations.
Then gently press along the fold
lines, slip the elastic band over
your head, and you'll be ready
for the adventure to start!

Anna loves colorful flowers!
Circle all the pink flowers above.
Which color flower
is your favorite?

Elsa

Queen Elsa might seem cold and uncaring, but it's only because she has a secret—she has the power to control ice and snow! Elsa needs to be guarded and controlled because she wants to protect her little sister, Anna, and the people of her kingdom.

Elsa can create snow and ice! How many snowflakes can you count? Circle the biggest.

Kristoff

Kristoff is the strong and silent type, and he likes to be by himself as much as possible—except for his loyal reindeer friend, Sven! Kristoff works hard on his ice business, and knows how to survive in the cold mountains.

Kristoff's best friend is a reindeer.
What's his name? Write it here.

· ·

What is your best friend's name?

Olaf

Olaf is a funny, loving, and trusting
snowman created by Queen Elsa. He's very
curious, and really wants to be helpful.
Olaf's biggest wish is to see summer—
he doesn't understand that he would
melt under the hot sun!

Olaf has a carrot for a nose!
Can you spot six more carrots
hidden around the page?

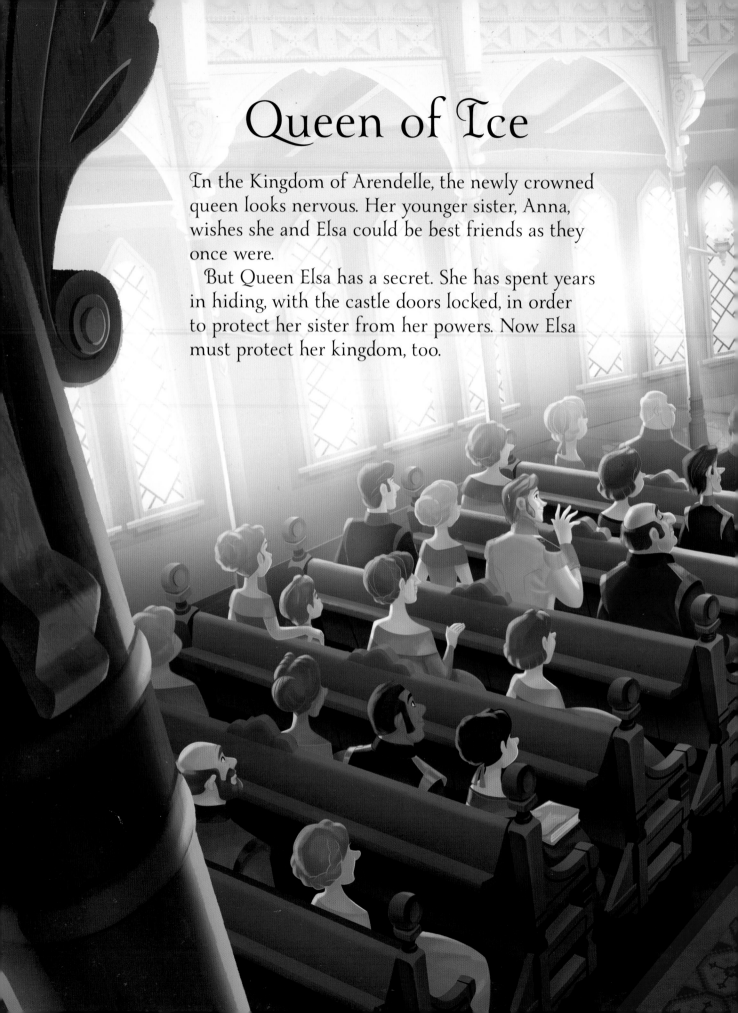

Queen of Ice

In the Kingdom of Arendelle, the newly crowned queen looks nervous. Her younger sister, Anna, wishes she and Elsa could be best friends as they once were.

But Queen Elsa has a secret. She has spent years in hiding, with the castle doors locked, in order to protect her sister from her powers. Now Elsa must protect her kingdom, too.

Join In

Put on the Elsa mask, and pretend it
is your coronation day. Use a chair as
your throne, and ask a friend to place
a tiara or headband on your head.
Then your friend must bow or curtsy!

When Elsa refuses to let Anna marry Hans—a prince she met only that day—the sisters argue. A blast of ice shoots across the room, and Elsa's secret is revealed. She can create snow and ice with her bare hands!

The townspeople watch, afraid, as Elsa flees from the castle. As she runs, everything she touches turns to ice.

Join In

Wearing your Elsa mask, pretend you can command snow and ice. Spread your fingers, then sweep your arms to make shapes in the air.

Join In

Put on the Kristoff mask.
Imagine you are talking to Sven,
and put on a goofy reindeer voice.
Talk to your own pet
if you have one.

Anna suddenly understands why Elsa remained hidden for so many years. With ice quickly spreading across the kingdom, she sets out to bring her sister back.

On her journey, Anna meets an ice harvester named Kristoff. She asks Kristoff to help her find Elsa and, finally, he agrees. Kristoff also introduces Anna to his trusty reindeer friend, Sven!

In their search for Elsa, Anna and Kristoff stumble across a spectacular winter wonderland. A little snowman named Olaf hops out from behind a tree to greet them. He is eager to help find Elsa, too, so that she can bring summer back to Arendelle. Anna and Kristoff don't have the heart to tell Olaf that summer isn't good for a snowman!

Join In

Put on the Olaf mask, and hop
from foot to foot. Now go and give
someone a lovely warm hug.
Olaf loves hugs!

Join In

Put on the Anna mask, and pretend Elsa
has blasted you with her icy powers.
Shiver as if you were really, really cold,
and wrap a blanket around
your shoulders.

At the top of a steep mountain, Queen Elsa is content to be alone in her ice palace, where she can't hurt anyone. She is not pleased when Anna turns up!

Elsa accidentally strikes Anna with an icy blow to the chest, and orders a giant snowman to chase the group off the mountain. Kristoff soon realizes that Anna is not well.... Elsa has put ice in her heart! Only an act of true love can save her now.

Guards seize Elsa and carry her back to Arendelle, locking her in a dungeon. Elsa escapes but soon comes face-to-face with the evil Prince Hans, who plans to rule Arendelle—by himself!

Anna quickly throws herself in front of Hans's sword to protect her sister and—*CLANK!* The blade shatters as Anna's body freezes to solid ice. The ice in her heart has spread.

Join In

Wearing the Anna mask, strike
a pose as you try to save Elsa.
Hold your pose for as long as
you can, as if you were frozen
on the spot!

Join In

Olaf is so excited to see his first summer!
Think of all the things you love
about summer—flowers, sunshine,
the beach.... Put on the Olaf mask,
and pretend you're experiencing
them for the first time.

Anna isn't frozen for long. Her act of true love for Elsa thaws her icy heart and body. At that moment, Elsa realizes love will bring back the summer!

The people of Arendelle cheer as the snow melts away. Elsa sends Hans back to his homeland, and makes a magic snow cloud to keep Olaf safe. Meanwhile, Anna surprises Kristoff with a kiss!

Join In

Put on your favorite mask, and ask your friends to wear the other masks. Pretend you're all skating on an ice rink. Twirl, spin, and leap across the ice. Just watch out for unsteady Sven!

With her powers under control, Elsa creates a huge ice rink inside the castle. Soon, everyone in the kingdom will arrive for a great skating celebration. The friends couldn't be happier—the sisters know they will be best friends forever, and Anna knows the doors of the castle will never be locked again.